Y0-BUW-344

My Little
Red Story Book

REVISED EDITION

- **ODILLE OUSLEY**
- **DAVID H. RUSSELL**

GINN AND COMPANY   BOSTON · NEW YORK · CHICAGO · ATLANTA
DALLAS · PALO ALTO · TORONTO · LONDON

Stories in This Book

660.8 H © Copyright, 1957, 1953, 1948, by Ginn and Company. Philippines Copyright, 1949, by Ginn and Company. All Rights Reserved

Tom

3

Ride, Tom.

Ride, ride.

Ride, Tom.

Tom ! Tom !

6

Betty

Ride, Betty.

Ride, Betty, ride.

Ride fast.

Ride fast, Betty.

Ride fast, Tom.

Ride fast.

Susan

Ride, Susan.

Ride, Bunny.

Ride fast, Susan.

Ride fast, Bunny.

Susan ! Susan !

See Bunny !

See Bunny, Susan.

Bunny! Bunny!

See Bunny, Tom.

See Bunny!

14

Flip

Tom! Betty!

See Flip and Bunny.

See Flip ride.

See Bunny ride.

Ride fast, Flip.

Ride fast, Bunny.

Ride and ride.

Bunny! Bunny!

Flip! Flip!

See Bunny and Flip!

Mother

Come, Betty.

Come, Tom.

Come, Betty and Tom.

Come and see.

Come, Betty.

Come, Tom.

Come and see Mother.

Come and see Mother.

Airplane ! Airplane !

See, Betty !

See, Susan !

Come and see.

The Airplane

Mother ! Mother !

Come and see Tom.

See the airplane, Mother.

See Tom and the airplane.

See Bunny, Mother.

Bunny can ride.

See Bunny ride.

Bunny can ride the airplane.

See the airplane, Susan.

Bunny can ride the airplane.

Bunny can ride fast.

Ride fast, Bunny.

Ride, Bunny, ride.

Pony

Father ! Father !

Come and see Pony.

See Tom ride.

Tom can ride Pony.

Tom can ride fast.

Come, Tom.

Come, come.

Come and see Father.

Come and see.

Father! Father!
See Tom ride Pony.
Tom can ride fast.

Ride, Tom, ride.
Ride Pony fast.

The Apple

Come, Tom.

See the apple.

Come and get the apple.

Get the apple, Tom.

Betty ! Betty !

See Tom and Pony.

See Tom get the apple.

Tom can get the apple.

Come, Pony.

Come and get the apple.

See Pony, Susan.

See Pony get the apple.

Susan and the Toys

Come, Betty.

Come fast.

Come and see Bunny.

Come and see the toys.

Come, Flip.

Come and see the toys.

Come and see Susan.

Come and see Bunny.

Betty! Betty!

Get Flip.

Get Flip, Tom.

Get Flip and the toys.

38

Tom and the Toys

Come, Betty.

See the toys.

See the apples.

Get the toys, Betty.

Get Bunny.

Get the airplane, Tom.

Get the apples.

The toys can ride.

The apples can ride.

Come fast, Tom.

Come fast!

Tom ! Tom !

See Bunny, Tom.

Get Bunny, Tom !

Get Bunny !

The Toys

Come, Mother.

Come, Betty and Susan.

Come and see.

Come and see Father.

Toys! Toys!

Get the toys, Betty.

Get the toys, Susan.

Get the airplane.

Get Bunny.

Father !   Father !

See the toys.

See the airplane.

See Bunny.

See the toys, Father !

Mother! Mother!

Come and see!

Come and see the toys.

And see Flip!

To the Teacher

My Little Red Story Book is the first Pre-Primer of the GINN BASIC READING SERIES. It is followed by Pre-Primer II, *My Little Green Story Book*, and Pre-Primer III, *My Little Blue Story Book*. This Pre-Primer introduces 19 words, 5 of which have already been presented in *Fun with Tom and Betty*, the Readiness book of this series. Only one new word is introduced on any page.

The lines in the list below indicate the ending of one story and the beginning of another.

New Words in This Book

3. Tom	18. . . .	33. . . .
4. ride	————	34. . . .
5. . . .	19. Mother	————
6. . . .	20. come	35. toys
————	21. . . .	36. . . .
7. Betty	22. airplane	37. . . .
8. . . .	————	38. . . .
9. . . .	23. the	————
10. fast	24. . . .	39. . . .
————	25. can	40. . . .
11. Susan	26. . . .	41. . . .
12. Bunny	————	42. . . .
13. see	27. Pony	————
14. . . .	28. Father	43. . . .
————	29. . . .	44. . . .
15. Flip	30. . . .	45. . . .
16. and	————	46. . . .
17. . . .	31. apple	47. . . .
	32. get	

ILLUSTRATIONS BY Ruth Steed